W9-COE-589

Richard Scarry's
BEST TIMES EVER
A Book About Seasons and Holidays

A GOLDEN BOOK · NEW YORK
Western Publishing Company, Inc., Racine, Wisconsin 53404

A Spring Celebration

It's springtime in Busytown. The days are getting warmer and flowers are in bloom. On May Day, Mother Cat has a party for Tom and his friends.

The children dance around the maypole and play outdoor games in the warm spring sunshine.

"London Bridge is falling down,"
sing the children as they go
under the bridge.

Go-Go and Pelican take turns tossing
beanbags. Whoops. Go-Go should aim better.

Wiggles and Flossie think it's a lovely day
for a game of croquet.

Haggis and Tom play happy music, and Big Hilda dances across the lawn like a ballerina. Flossie loves to watch Hilda dance.

The children join hands and dance around in a circle. "This is the best May Day ever," says Tom.

A Holiday Picnic

Summer brings hot sunny days.
The piglets love summer because
they can play outside all day long.
Today is the Fourth of July,
and the piglets are very excited.
Mother and Father Pig are
taking them to the park
for a special picnic.

The kittens love to go down the slide and ride the merry-go-round. The piglets love piggyback rides from Mother and Father Pig.

In the early evening the Pig family decides to take a boat ride on the lake. Out in the middle the pigs have a delicious snack of watermelon.

"Look," says Polly Pig. "The fireworks are starting!"

"This is the best Fourth of July picnic ever," exclaim the piglets.

Summer Vacation

August is a good time for a summer vacation. The Bear family is going on a trip to the seashore. Look at all the things the bears have packed!

At the beach Father Bear teaches Little Sister how to swim.

Huckle is building a big sand castle. Watch out for that wave, Huckle!

On the way home the Bear family visits Wild West Park.

"Hello," says the sheriff as he waves to Huckle. "Are you having fun?"

"Yes," says Huckle. "This is my favorite summer vacation ever."

Autumn Fun and Feasting

After the summer, the air grows cool and fall arrives. Father Pig takes some of the piglets to a farm stand where they buy good things from the harvest.

"Mmmm, this apple is delicious," says Father Pig as he eats a freshly picked apple.

In late November the Pig family prepares for Thanksgiving. Mother Pig takes some of the piglets to the market to buy groceries for their Thanksgiving meal.

Mother Pig has cooked a wonderful Thanksgiving dinner. There is so much delicious food that Baby Piglet can't wait to begin.

"We have many things to be thankful for," says Father Pig. "Happy Thanksgiving, everyone!"

Winter's Happy Days and Holidays

The first snows of winter have fallen, making everything look beautiful. The Cat family is enjoying a sleigh ride through the snow-covered fields.

Everywhere you look, children
are playing winter games.

December is a time of happy holidays and family fun. On Christmas morning the Bunny family goes to visit Grandma and Grandpa Bunny. The bunnies are carrying lots of presents. Grandpa and Grandma will be so happy!

Look! There's the Cat family. They are visiting relatives for Christmas, too.

Look at all those happy faces.
You can see that this will be
the cats' happiest Christmas ever.

*7.95

DATE DUE

8/4			
	1995		

∅ 7.95